Contents

Material in this edition was previously published by
Ladybird Books in *Stories for Bedtime*.

Ladybird books are widely available, but in case of difficulty
may be ordered by post or telephone from:
Ladybird Books – Cash Sales Department Littlegate Road
Paignton Devon TQ3 3BE · Telephone 0803 554761

A catalogue record for this book is available from the British Library

Published by Ladybird Books Ltd Loughborough Leicestershire UK
Ladybird Books Inc Auburn Maine 04210 USA

Ladybird

FAIRY TALES

Retold by BRIAN MORSE
Illustrated by PETER STEVENSON

The Twelve Dancing Princesses

There was once a handsome young man called Michael whose job was looking after the villagers' cows. All the local girls thought he was marvellous, but Michael didn't want to marry one of them. Come what may, he was determined to marry a princess.

Then one day a beautiful lady came to him in a dream. "Michael," she said, "go to the castle of Belœil. Find your princess there."

When he told the villagers, they jeered, "Cowherds don't marry princesses!" But Michael believed his dream. Next morning he set off to seek his fortune.

As it happened, he couldn't have gone to the castle at a better time, for something strange was happening there. The King's twelve beautiful daughters all slept in the same room, which was locked and bolted each night at bedtime. Yet in the morning the Princesses were as tired as if they'd been up all night. Even more mysteriously, the soles of their dancing shoes were worn out each morning.

The Princesses said, "All we do is sleep!"

But the King didn't believe that. He announced that if any prince discovered their secret, he could choose one of the Princesses for his bride. Prince after prince had been locked in with the Princesses. None of them had ever been seen again.

When he reached the castle, Michael got a job as a gardener. One of his duties was to give the Princesses a bouquet of flowers each morning. As soon as Michael set eyes on the youngest Princess, he knew that she was the one for him. He could tell she liked the look of him too, even though he was only a gardener.

That night he had another dream. The lady told him to plant two trees. When they grew they would grant him any wish.

Strangely enough, two young trees were by his side when he woke. He planted them and as soon as they'd grown, he said, "Make me invisible!"

His wish was granted. That night the invisible Michael hid in the Princesses' room. As soon as the door had been locked, the Princesses put on their party clothes.

Then the eldest clapped her hands three times and a trap door opened. Down a hidden staircase the Princesses went, with Michael following, but carelessly he stepped on the hem of the youngest Princess's dress.

Frightened, she called, "Someone is holding my dress!"

"Silly!" her eldest sister called back. "It caught on a nail."

At the bottom of the staircase was a grove of beautiful trees with silver-spangled leaves. Beyond that was another with gold-spangled leaves, then another where the leaves were studded with diamonds.

At last they reached a lake where twelve boats waited. On the far side was a castle. Michael climbed into the youngest Princess's boat.

"Hurry! We're getting left behind," she complained to the Prince who was rowing it. (He was one of the Princes who'd so mysteriously disappeared.)

"It seems heavier tonight," the poor Prince said, rowing his hardest.

In the castle, a ball was in full swing. All night Michael watched the youngest Princess dancing. How lovely she was! How beautifully she danced!

At three in the morning, the Princesses' dancing shoes were worn out. Back across the lake they were rowed. As they passed through the grove of silver-spangled leaves, Michael snapped off a spray of them.

In the morning Michael pushed the spray into the youngest Princess's bouquet. She saw it but said nothing.

The second night Michael followed again. Next morning the youngest Princess saw a sprig of gold-spangled leaves in her bouquet.

"You know our secret!" she said to Michael. She offered him gold not to tell the King. Michael refused it. In desperation the youngest Princess told her sisters.

"Throw him in a dungeon!" they said. But the youngest Princess said, "No!"

"Then let your gardener come with us," the sisters said. "We'll drug him like the others."

That night Michael had no need to wish himself invisible. Instead he wished for a magnificent suit of clothes so that he could look like a prince. He went with the Princesses to the ball and danced all night. Then, while they were resting, the eldest brought him a glass of drugged wine.

Now, Michael had heard all about this plot when he was invisible, but he could not bear to be parted from the youngest Princess, so he put the glass to his lips. He was about to drink, when she knocked it out of his hand.

"I don't want you to be like the others!" she cried. "I want us to live in the everyday world, even if it *does* mean I become a gardener's wife!" Bursting into tears, she threw herself into Michael's arms.

All at once, it was as though a spell had been broken. The real Princes suddenly remembered who they were and immediately asked the other Princesses to marry them. The Princesses had been enchanted by the magical world they had visited so often, but now they were overjoyed to find real happiness at last.

But the story ends even more happily than that, for when the King heard how Michael had broken the spell, he made him a prince too. So the youngest Princess didn't have to marry a gardener after all!

Rapunzel

Once a man and his wife longed and longed for a child of their own. Then at last the wife discovered that she was expecting a baby.

One day the wife was standing at a high window, gazing down into a neighbouring garden full of beautiful flowers and vegetables, when her eye fell on a bed of special lettuces. Immediately it was as if a spell had been put on her. She could think of nothing else.

"I have to have some of that lettuce or I'll die," she told herself. She stopped eating and began to waste away.

Eventually her husband grew so worried that, one evening, he climbed over the wall into the neighbouring garden and picked a handful of lettuce leaves. This was a very brave thing to do, as the garden belonged to a powerful witch.

His wife ate the lettuce greedily, but the handful wasn't enough. Her husband had to go back next evening. This time the witch was lying in wait for him.

"How dare you sneak in and steal from me!" she screeched. "You will pay for this!"

The husband begged to be forgiven. He explained how badly his wife needed the lettuce.

"In that case," the witch said more softly, "take as much as she wants. But when the baby is born, you must give it to me." The husband was so terrified that he agreed.

A few weeks later the baby arrived. That same day, the witch came to take away the newborn child. She called her Rapunzel because that was the name of the kind of lettuce that the mother had wanted so badly.

The witch cared for the little girl well. When Rapunzel was twelve years old, she was the most beautiful child in the world. Then the witch took her to a high tower in the middle of a forest. This tower had no stair, just a tiny window at the top.

When the witch wanted to visit, she called, "Rapunzel! Rapunzel! Let down your golden hair!" and Rapunzel would hold her long, braided hair over the windowsill for the witch to climb.

This went on for several years, until one day a king's son came hunting in the forest. From far away he heard the sound of a lovely voice singing. He rode here and there among the trees until he came to the tower but he could see no way up it.

Haunted by the voice, he came back again and again until one day he saw the witch and watched how she got into the tower. Next day as it was growing dark, he called out softly, "Rapunzel! Rapunzel! Let down your golden hair!" A minute later he was with the girl.

At first Rapunzel was frightened, for she had never had any visitors except the witch, but the Prince gently explained how he'd heard her singing and fallen in love with her voice. When she felt less afraid, he asked her to marry him, and blushing, Rapunzel agreed.

But how was Rapunzel to escape? The clever girl had a brilliant idea. The Prince must bring skeins of silk each time he visited. Rapunzel could make them into her own ladder.

All went well and the witch noticed nothing until one day, without thinking, Rapunzel said, "Mother, why is it easier for the Prince to climb up my hair than you?" Then the truth was out.

"You wicked girl! How you have deceived me! I meant to keep you free of the world's evil," the witch raved. She caught hold of Rapunzel and cut off her hair, then sent her to live in a faraway desert place.

That same night, the witch lay in wait for the Prince. When he called out, "Rapunzel! Rapunzel! Let down your golden hair!" she let down the girl's chopped-off hair and hauled him up. The Prince was at her mercy.

"The cat has taken the bird," the witch hissed. "She'll sing no more for you."

In despair the Prince threw himself from the window. He wasn't killed, but the brambles below scratched his eyes. For several years he wandered blindly through the forest, weeping for his lost Rapunzel and living on roots and berries.

Then one day he reached the desert place where Rapunzel was living. Far off he heard a sweet voice singing.

"Rapunzel! Rapunzel!" he called. Rapunzel cried with joy at seeing her Prince again, and two of her tears fell on his eyes. A miracle happened, and the Prince could see again.

The happy couple travelled back to the Prince's kingdom, where they were received with great joy and lived happily ever after.

The Princess and the Pea

Princes *must* marry princesses. There's no point in them falling in love with ordinary girls, however pretty they are. Everyone knows that, especially princes.

Once there was a prince who desperately wanted to get married. But, poor thing, he couldn't find the right princess. His mother and father the King and Queen did their best to help him. They even took their summer holidays in places where they met lots of princesses. When they got back they'd say, "Oh, by the way, we saw this lovely girl." The Prince would smile and say, "I bet she's a princess." And his parents would reply, "How did you guess? We've got her address. Why don't we invite her for a weekend?"

Unfortunately, the Prince never managed to fall in love. He *almost* fell in love. In fact, once he was engaged for over a year to a princess from Transylvania, but in the end the engagement was called off. Quite right too. They would never have lived happily ever after.

One dark November day a storm blew up. The wind lashed the palace roof so hard that tiles blew off like a storm of confetti. Trees in the royal park were uprooted, and the river burst its banks. It was so gloomy that the lights had to be put on by half past three (the King hated wasting candles), and it was so cold that the fires had to be banked right up. And the rain! It bucketed down. Not even the royal dogs, who lay sorrowfully in their baskets dreaming of sunshine and rabbits, wanted to go out.

About eight o'clock there was a knock at the palace door. A servant was sent. He came back and whispered something in the King's ear.

"Who says she's a princess?" the King asked, surprised.

"The young lady at the door says so, Sire," the servant said. "She says she lost her way. She's soaked through."

"A princess out in this weather? Whatever next?" exclaimed the King. "Oh well, I'd better come."

But the Prince was there before him. He was already on his knees before a most elegant young lady. In fact, he was on the point of asking her to marry him! Luckily the Queen arrived in the nick of time and whisked the young lady away to change her wet things.

"Well?" the King said, when the Queen came back downstairs. "Is she a princess? I bet she's just a pop star or a prime minister's daughter like all the other girls he falls in love with. I'm beginning to hate the word 'princess'. I didn't have so much trouble falling in love with a princess in *my* day." He smiled fondly at the Queen.

"I think I'll have to give her the test," the Queen said, "and hope she passes."

"Test?" queried the King. The Queen explained. "A pea? How can you tell if she's a princess with a pea?" puzzled the King.

"You just wait till morning," the Queen said, smiling.

Next morning the King paced up and down the sunlit breakfast room. "Isn't she up yet?" he asked his wife. "I hate people who lie in bed all day."

"Patience," said the Queen. "Let's see if my little plan has worked."

At last the young lady appeared. The King gasped. She looked awful, as if she'd never gone to bed at all. The Prince rushed up to her. "Darling! What's the matter?" he said. "Mother, didn't you give her our softest bed?"

"Of course I did," replied the Queen. "I put twenty mattresses one on top of the other, then twenty eiderdown quilts on top of them. What could be softer than that?"

"I feel black and blue all over," the young lady complained, as she dropped into a chair. "I'm covered with bruises the size of potatoes. That was the most uncomfortable bed I have *ever* slept in."

When he heard that, the Prince turned pale with fright. What if she left the palace and he never saw her again?

"But I did get a little sleep eventually," the young lady went on. "About four o'clock I couldn't stand it any longer, so I got out of bed and felt under the mattresses. You won't believe what I found." She held something out on the palm of her hand.

"A pea?" said the Prince. "Who left that there? I'll have their head off!"

"A pea!" said the King happily. "I understand now. Only a princess would be kept awake by a pea under her mattress!"

"Twenty mattresses," his wife reminded him.

So the Prince and Princess were married and lived a long and happy life together. And every night before they went to bed the Prince, even when he was King, checked under the mattress to make sure that no one had put even the tiniest pea there.

Cinderella

There was once a girl whose mother had died. When her father remarried, his new wife brought the two daughters from her first marriage to the house.

These daughters took an instant dislike to their new sister. They threw everything out of her room into the attic. Instead of treating her like a sister, they made her do all the work.

Even when she'd finished her jobs, she wasn't allowed to join the rest of the family. Instead she had to spend her evenings by the dying kitchen fire, warming her hands above the cinders – which is how she came to be called "Cinderella".

One day, however, the stepsisters received an invitation to a ball at the palace. They were thrilled. Everyone knew that the Prince wanted to get married. Perhaps he would choose one of the ladies at the ball for his wife!

The two sisters immediately set about making themselves as beautiful as possible. Unfortunately this was very difficult as, unlike Cinderella, they were rather ugly!

On the evening of the ball, when her stepsisters had driven off, Cinderella sat in the kitchen quietly crying to herself. "What's the matter, Cinderella?" a voice asked.

Cinderella sobbed, "I wish I could go to the ball myself."

"And so you shall," the voice said. Cinderella looked up, startled.

A beautiful lady was standing beside her.

"I'm your fairy godmother," she said. "Now, no time to waste! Fetch me a pumpkin!"

Cinderella did as she was told. Her godmother touched the pumpkin with her wand, and it turned into a golden coach.

"Now six mice…" Cinderella fetched them and her godmother turned them into horses to pull the coach.

"A rat…" She turned that into a coachman.

"And six lizards…" She turned them into footmen to run behind the coach.

Last it was Cinderella's turn. One touch of the wand and her rags became a dress so magnificent it took your breath away. On her feet glittered a pair of glass slippers.

"One word of warning, though," her godmother said. "Be home by midnight. At twelve o'clock your dress will turn back to rags, your coach to a pumpkin, your horses to mice. You don't want the Prince to see that, do you? Now, off you go and enjoy yourself."

That night Cinderella was the belle of the ball. The ladies (especially her two stepsisters) admired her dress and begged her for the name of her dressmaker. The gentlemen all wanted to kiss her hand and dance with her.

But the Prince fell in love with her at first sight! No one else was allowed to dance with her after that.

The minutes whirled away and it was only when the clock began to strike twelve that Cinderella remembered she should be home.

"Come back!" the Prince called, but away she ran. By the time she reached the street, her dress was rags again. All she had left was one of the glass slippers. The other was lost, she didn't know where.

That night Cinderella cried herself to sleep. She knew that life would never be so marvellous again.

But that wasn't true. The other slipper had been found on the palace steps. Next morning the Prince went round the town from house to house, begging ladies to try it on. "If I don't find the beautiful stranger who wore it last night, I'll die," he said.

At last he reached Cinderella's house. The two stepsisters tried it on. No use. It just didn't fit.

Brokenhearted, for there were only a few houses left, the Prince was about to leave when he noticed the serving-girl.

"Madam," he said gallantly, "why don't you try it too?"

"Her? Don't be silly!" the stepsisters cried.

But the Prince insisted. He'd seen how beautiful Cinderella was. And of course the shoe fitted her perfectly. Spitting with rage and jealousy, the two sisters could only look on as the Prince knelt and asked Cinderella to marry him. And she did, of course!

Beauty and the Beast

Once there was a rich merchant who had three daughters. Two of them were totally selfish, but the third, Beauty, was kind and loving.

One day the merchant received news that his ships had sunk in a great storm. He had lost all his money and was left with nothing but a tiny cottage in the country. The two greedy sisters hated it. They refused to do anything except lie in bed and moan. All the work was left to Beauty.

After a time, however, the merchant heard that one of his missing ships had reached port. Before he set off to claim it, he asked his daughters what presents they'd like him to bring back. The greedy sisters cheered up straightaway.

"Dresses and jewels!" they begged.

"And you, Beauty?" the merchant asked.

"A rose. That will be enough for me," Beauty said.

A few days later, the merchant sadly began his ride home. He was as poor as ever, for he had been cheated out of his money. As he entered a forest, the night drew in. It was dark and cold. A blizzard blew and the snow piled into drifts. Wolves howled in the distance.

For hours the merchant and his horse stumbled about, lost, until suddenly, straight ahead, a bright light shone from a magnificent castle. But this was the strangest of castles, for although there were fires in the grates and lights burnt in every room, no one was about. The merchant called and called. No one came. Eventually he tethered his tired horse in the stables and sat down at the castle's high table to eat the meal laid out there. Then he went to bed.

22

In the morning, he found new clothes laid out for him. Downstairs a cup of steaming hot chocolate had been put out for his breakfast.

"This castle must belong to a good fairy who has taken pity on me," the merchant said. "If only I could thank her."

As he was leaving, the merchant passed a bed of roses. "At least I can keep my promise to Beauty," he thought. He snapped off a stem of blossoms. Immediately there was a bellow of rage. From behind the bushes leapt a terrible beast, so ugly that the merchant almost fainted.

"You ungrateful man!" the Beast roared. "I saved your life! I fed and clothed you! Now you steal my beautiful roses. You must die at once!"

The merchant fell to his knees. "That rose was for one of my daughters, my lord," he said.

"I am no lord, I am a Beast," the creature snarled. He towered over the merchant. "And as for your precious daughters, go and see if one of them will save your life by coming to live with me. If not, in three months you will die."

The merchant rode home sorrowfully through the sunlit forest. At home the two sisters paid hardly any attention to the story of his terrible adventure. They were infuriated that he'd brought them no dresses or jewels. But Beauty was different.

"Father, let me go," she begged.

"You deserve to," the sisters said. "If it hadn't been for your stupid rose, the Beast wouldn't have wanted to kill our father."

Three months later the merchant returned to the castle with Beauty. All was as before: the empty castle, the meal ready on the table. Then, when they'd finished eating, the Beast appeared. Beauty trembled, for he was as dreadful as her father had described, or worse!

"Have you come here of your own free will?" the Beast demanded.

"Yes," Beauty replied.

"In that case your father must leave in the morning and never set foot here again."

So next morning Beauty was left alone. At first she cried, but then she remembered a dream she'd had. In it a lady had told her, "Beauty, your bravery in saving your father will be rewarded."

Beauty cheered up. Perhaps after all things might go well. She walked through the gardens, looking sadly at the rose beds, then explored inside the castle. Imagine her surprise when she found a door with her name on it. Inside, the room was exactly as she'd have furnished it herself, full of books and musical instruments.

"The Beast cannot mean to harm me," she thought, "if he intends me to enjoy myself so much."

Beauty took out a book. On it was written in letters of gold, "Here you are Queen. Your wish is my command."

"If only I could see what my father is doing now!" she cried out loud. And she could – in the mirror on the far side of the room. As the picture faded, Beauty felt less lonely and homesick.

That night at supper, the Beast appeared. "Beauty," he asked timidly, "may I watch you?"

"You are master here," Beauty said.

"No," the Beast replied. "You are the mistress. I will go if you wish." The Beast hesitated. "But tell me, do you find me unbearably ugly?"

Beauty didn't know what to say, then looked him straight in the face. "Beast, I have to tell the truth. I'm afraid I do."

When she had finished her meal, the Beast had one more question. "Beauty," he asked, "will you marry me?"

"No, Beast, never."

The sigh the Beast gave echoed round the castle.

Every night at nine o'clock, the Beast came to talk. Beauty found she liked him more and more. She even fretted if he was late. If only he wasn't so ugly! If only he wouldn't keep asking her to marry him! She dreaded having to refuse and hearing the haunting sigh he gave afterwards.

"You may not love me, Beauty," he said, "but you'll never leave me, will you? Promise that." For three months it went on like this.

Then one day Beauty saw in the mirror that her father was ill. At once she asked the Beast if she could go home to nurse him.

"Beauty, you must go," the Beast replied. "You know that I will die of grief if you don't come back, don't you? I am afraid that you will stay at your father's, but if you want to come back, just put your ring on your bedside table. The next morning you will wake in my castle."

"I will return in a week," Beauty promised.

Next morning Beauty woke in her own warm bed in her father's cottage. How overjoyed he was to see her! It made him better at once. That afternoon her sisters, who had both got married in the meantime, came round to visit. How jealous and angry they were when they saw that their father's favourite had come back.

"Listen!" one said to the other. "Let's trick her. Let's persuade her to stay a second week. Then the Beast will come and kill her." Instead of moaning and criticizing her, the two sisters rubbed onions in their eyes and pretended to cry at the thought of Beauty leaving. Beauty promised to stay another week.

Yet soon Beauty found that she was missing the Beast as much as she'd missed her father. As she slept she had a terrible dream, in which the Beast was lying cold and lifeless on the castle lawn. She sat bolt upright in bed. How could she have been so heartless? Quickly she pulled off her ring and put it on the bedside table. When she woke again, she was in the Beast's castle.

That evening she waited for him. Nine o'clock struck. He didn't come. Quarter past struck too. Suddenly full of dread, she ran through the castle and out into the gardens. The Beast lay on the lawn. She had killed him! Forgetting his appearance, Beauty threw herself upon him. His heart was still beating!

"I thought you would never come back. I tried to starve myself to death," he whispered.

"But I love you, Beast!" Beauty said. "I want to marry you."

Then something amazing happened. The castle seemed to become even more beautiful, more full of light. Beauty gazed around, then turned back to the Beast. But the Beast had gone. In his place a handsome young prince lay on the lawn.

"I want the Beast," Beauty cried. The Prince stood up.

"I *am* the Beast," he said. "An evil fairy put a spell on me. She turned me into something unbearably ugly. I would have stayed like that for the rest of my life, if you had not said you would marry me."

The Prince led Beauty into the castle. There she found her father and the lady she'd seen in her dream, the good fairy.

"Beauty," the good fairy said, "you have got your reward."

She waved her wand. In an instant everyone in the hall was transported to the Prince's kingdom, where the Prince's subjects greeted him with cheers and applause. Soon Beauty and her Beast were married. They became the happiest Prince and Princess that ever lived.

29

Snow White

The snow lay deep on the ground. At a window of the palace the Queen sat sewing and dreaming. As she sewed, her needle pricked her finger and three bright drops of blood fell onto her embroidery.

The Queen looked at the drops and suddenly she had a lovely thought. "If my baby is a daughter, I want her to be as white as snow, as red as blood and as black as the frame of this window," she said.

Not long after that she gave birth. Her daughter was exactly as she'd imagined her. They called the baby Snow White, but sadly her mother died within a few hours of her birth.

A year later the King remarried. The new Queen was very beautiful but so proud that she couldn't bear the thought of anyone being more beautiful than herself. In her room she had a magic mirror. She would stare into it for hours on end and ask,

> *"Mirror, mirror, on the wall,*
> *Am I the fairest of them all?"*

Without fail the mirror answered, *"Yes, O Queen."*

But one day, when Snow White was fourteen years old, the mirror said,

> *"No, O Queen, you no longer are.*
> *Snow White is more beautiful by far."*

The Queen was so angry and upset that she couldn't sleep or eat. What was she to do? Then she made up her mind. She sent for the royal huntsman.

"Take Snow White into the forest and kill her. Bring back her heart and liver to prove she's dead."

The huntsman led Snow White away, but when he drew his knife the girl began to cry. He couldn't kill her. "Anyway," he thought, as she ran away among the trees, "before night comes a wolf or bear will do my job for me."

A young boar came by, so the huntsman killed that instead and took its heart and liver back to the Queen. The evil woman boiled them with salt and ate them and never knew the difference.

But Snow White wasn't killed by a wolf or a bear. As night fell she came to a little house on the other side of the mountains. She knocked, but no one answered. Plucking up courage, she went inside.

Here was a sight to cheer her up – a long table with seven places set and a row of seven beds along the wall. Still no one came, and Snow White was so tired and hungry that she took a spoonful from each plate and lay down to sleep on the seventh bed.

A little later the house's owners returned. They were seven dwarfs who worked in a silver mine deep under the mountains.

"What a beautiful child!" they said, when they saw Snow White.

When she woke in the morning, Snow White was terrified by the sight of the little men, but she soon learnt how kind-hearted they were. They asked her to keep house for them, and she agreed at once.

"Take care," said the dwarfs as they set off for work. "And don't open the door. One day your stepmother will find out that you're here and again try to kill you."

And very soon the Queen did go to her mirror. Imagine her horror when it said,

"O Queen, you are the fairest here,
But on the far side of the high mountains' wall,
In the dwarfs' neat and tidy home,
Snow White is still the fairest of them all."

Immediately the Queen sprang into action. Dressed as an old pedlar woman, she set off across the mountains with a tray of ribbons.

"Pretty things to buy!" she called, and knocked at the dwarfs' door. Snow White, who was looking out of the window, fell in love with the lovely ribbon the old lady held up. What harm could there be? She opened the door.

"This one, my pretty?" the Queen asked, as she fastened it round Snow White's neck and twisted and twisted. Snow White fell down as if she were dead.

And that is how the dwarfs found her that night. They cut the ribbon and slowly Snow White came back to life. It was her second escape.

Next morning the Queen went to her mirror. How angry she was when she found that Snow White was still alive. She disguised herself again and set off across the mountains.

"Pretty things to buy!" she called by the dwarfs' door. When Snow White saw the comb the old woman was holding up, she forgot all about the danger. She opened the door.

"Your hair is so beautiful, let me comb it for you," the Queen said. But the comb was poisoned, and Snow White fell down as if dead. That night the dwarfs removed the comb and brought Snow White back to life again. That was her third escape.

When the Queen went to her mirror next day, she found Snow White was still alive, and her fury knew no bounds. This time she knew that she would need her most devilish magic. She prepared an apple that was poisonous on one side only. This time she set off disguised as an old beggar woman.

"An apple for the pretty young lady?" called the Queen under Snow White's window. "It's free. No need to come to the door. I'll pass it through the window."

She saw Snow White hesitate. "Not worried it's bad, are you?" The Queen bit into the side that wasn't poisoned. "See, it's perfect." She passed the rosy apple to Snow White.

The moment Snow White bit into the poison, she fell to the ground.

The Queen peered in through the window. "Well, that's the end of you, my beauty," she said, "and good riddance." Off home she went. And next time she looked in her mirror it told her that, yes, she was the fairest of them all. How happy she was!

This time none of the dwarfs' skills could bring Snow White back to life. After three days they lost all hope, but strangely she still looked alive. Instead of burying her, they put her in a glass coffin and set it on top of a high hill.

Some time later a prince came to stay with the dwarfs. He saw Snow White in her coffin and immediately fell in love with her.

"Let me take the coffin back to my palace or I'll die," he begged the dwarfs.

The little men took pity on him, and agreed. But as the Prince's servants lifted the coffin, the piece of poisoned apple that had stuck in Snow White's throat was dislodged. She sat up, wondering where she was, and the first thing she saw was the handsome young Prince. It was love at first sight. Within a few weeks she and the Prince were engaged to be married.

One of the wedding guests was Snow White's stepmother. As soon as she entered the room, she recognized Snow White, but this time she was powerless. The servants seized her and the Prince banished her to a faraway land where she could do no more harm. From that day on, Snow White was the happiest girl in the kingdom as well as the most beautiful.

Thumbelina

Once a young wife longed and longed for a little girl of her own. Finally she got all her money together and went to a witch to ask for help.

"Is that all she gave you? That's just an ordinary barleycorn!" her husband grumbled when she got home. But the wife knew better. She planted the barleycorn and after a time it grew into a beautiful red and yellow tulip. Leaning forward, she kissed the petals softly. Very slowly and gently they opened out. And there, sitting inside the flower, was a tiny little girl. The wife loved her the moment she saw her.

Because the little girl was so small, only half as tall as a grown-up's thumb, the wife named her Thumbelina.

No one could have looked after Thumbelina better. The young wife gave her half a walnut shell for a bed, the petals of a violet for a mattress, and a rose petal for a blanket. When she wasn't sleeping, Thumbelina played on the table or listened to her mother's stories. She was very happy.

But one dark night, an old mother toad crept in through a broken windowpane and stole the little girl. "What a lovely wife she'll make you!" the toad croaked to her son, who was sitting on a lily pad in the middle of the stream. "Kark! Kark! Brek-kek-bex!" the son croaked back. He was as happy as could be at the thought of marrying Thumbelina.

But the little girl was very unhappy. "Please take me home!" she cried. One day, while the toads were away getting ready for the wedding, a shoal of minnows heard Thumbelina crying. They popped their heads out of the water. "Please help me," the little girl sobbed. The fish thought she was so beautiful that they gnawed through the root of the lily pad. It floated away down the stream.

For a week Thumbelina travelled along as happy as could be, enchanted by the wonderful sights she saw. But one day a flying beetle swooped over the water, saw how beautiful she was, and snatched her up. In great excitement, he flew to the top of a tree and called all the other beetles to come and look.

"We're going to get married!" he squeaked. "Us!"

But the other beetles, especially the ladies, didn't think much of Thumbelina at all. "Ugh! She's ugly! She's only got two legs! Where are her feelers?" they mocked. "She looks like a human!" In the end, the beetle got so tired of being laughed at for wanting to marry Thumbelina that he dropped her in a daisy.

For the rest of the summer and all of the autumn, Thumbelina lived on her own. She wove a hammock to sleep in from blades of grass and hung it under a shamrock. She took nectar from the flowers for food and drank the dew when she was thirsty. But then cold winter came. The birds flew away. The leaves fell off the trees. The shamrock shrivelled and died.

One day it began to snow. For tiny Thumbelina, each snowflake was like a shovelful of snow thrown in her face. She wrapped herself in a leaf to keep warm but it hardly made any difference. As she searched desperately for somewhere to shelter, an old fieldmouse took pity on her and called her into her nest.

"You can stay with me if you do the housework and tell me stories," the fieldmouse said. So Thumbelina was safe and happy again, until one day the fieldmouse's friend, a mole, came visiting. Then things changed. When he heard Thumbelina singing as she did the housework, the blind mole fell in love with her too.

"Come and see my house," he squeaked. "It's twenty times bigger than this."

Of course, the mole lived underground, at the end of a long, dark tunnel. He was used to never seeing the sky or the sun, but Thumbelina hated it.

"Just wait till you get there. You'll want to marry me straightaway," the mole panted, as he led Thumbelina and the fieldmouse deeper and deeper under the earth. Then Thumbelina stumbled over something on the tunnel floor.

"Never mind that," the mole called. "That died long ago." But Thumbelina stopped. She felt cold feathers. It was a dead bird. How sad! She put her ear to the bird's chest and just as the bossy mole shouted, "Hurry along! We'll be there soon!", Thumbelina felt the tiny flutter of the bird's heart.

The bird was a swallow who had hurt his wing and been left behind when the other birds flew south at the end of summer. All winter Thumbelina crept down the dark tunnel to take the swallow food and water. Slowly she nursed him back to health.

On the first day of spring, the swallow was well enough to join his friends who had flown back from the warm south. How sad Thumbelina was to see him go. The swallow had been her one true friend.

"At the end of summer," the fieldmouse said that night, "you and my friend the mole shall get married, Thumbelina. Your room is almost ready. The spiders are spinning your sheets at this very moment."

All too soon the summer had passed. On the day before the wedding, Thumbelina walked through the fields saying goodbye to the sun and the sky and all the things she'd never see again. She was quietly crying to herself when a voice above her called her name. Thumbelina looked up. It was her friend, the swallow!

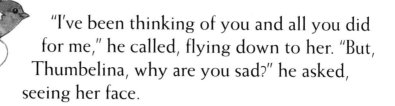

"I've been thinking of you and all you did for me," he called, flying down to her. "But, Thumbelina, why are you sad?" he asked, seeing her face.

Thumbelina explained about the mole and the wedding. "Marry the mole? You don't have to do that!" the swallow cried in horror. "Climb onto my back! Come south with me and my friends. That's right – catch hold of my feathers. You're so small you won't hurt."

So, safe on the swallow's back, Thumbelina flew south. Sometimes they soared high over icy mountains, sometimes they skimmed low over plains and sandy deserts. Once they crossed a stormy sea and the spray from the waves reached up and splashed them. But all the time the air grew warmer, until one day they arrived at a place where there were many swallows' nests. Below, at the bottom of a cliff, was a field of beautiful flowers. The swallow gently put Thumbelina down on one of them.

"You'll be happy here," he said. "I know."

But Thumbelina felt sad. "Here I am again, sitting in a flower!" she thought as her friend flew away.

But what did she see before her? A young man, exactly the same size as her, was smiling at her from the nearest flower!

"You are the most beautiful girl I've ever seen," he said, and he called out to his friends. A thousand other fairies appeared among the flowers to welcome Thumbelina.

Within a month, the young man and Thumbelina were married and became the King and Queen of all the fairies. Little Thumbelina was happy at last.

Sleeping Beauty

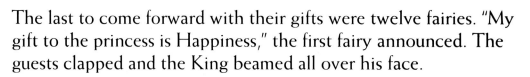

Once a king and queen gave an enormous party to celebrate the birth of their daughter. After the feast the King told everyone how happy he was to be a father, for he and his wife had been waiting for years to have a child. Next he made everyone laugh with his story about learning to change nappies. Then it was time for the guests to give the baby princess their presents.

The last to come forward with their gifts were twelve fairies. "My gift to the princess is Happiness," the first fairy announced. The guests clapped and the King beamed all over his face.

"Mine is Beauty," said the second. "Mine Wisdom," said the third. And so they went on.

42

The twelfth fairy was about to give her gift when a clap of thunder shook the palace. The doors burst open and the guests cowered as an old woman shuffled in.

"The thirteenth fairy!" people gasped in horror.

The fairy's terrible voice hissed from the doorway, "Where's my invitation, King?"

"Someone must have forgotten to deliver it," the King mumbled. "Servants! Set another place! Quick!" Actually he hadn't invited her because he only had twelve golden plates for the fairies to eat from, so he'd decided to leave one out.

The fairy stood over the little princess's cradle. The baby gurgled and reached up her tiny hand. Suddenly the fairy cackled, "My gift is that on the princess's fifteenth birthday she will prick her finger on a spindle and die!"

With another clap of thunder the wicked fairy flew away. The palace doors banged shut. There was a terrible silence. Then the Queen began to cry.

The twelfth fairy stepped forward. "I have not given my present yet," she said softly. "I can't undo the evil spell, but I can change it. My gift will be that instead of dying, the princess will sleep for a hundred years."

Years passed and all went well. The baby grew into a healthy young girl, pretty and happy and clever. The King and Queen no longer thought about the evil spell. All the spindles in the land had long been destroyed. Surely the princess was safe.

But on the very day of her fifteenth birthday, the princess found a door she'd never noticed before. Behind it a staircase climbed into a tower. Up the princess went until she reached a door with a golden key. The princess entered a tiny room. An old lady sat at a wheel. "What are you doing?" the princess asked. The old lady smiled. "I'm spinning! Don't stand there staring, child. Try it yourself." She pushed the spindle towards the princess.

At that moment a terrible thing happened. The sharp spindle pricked the princess's finger and she sank to the floor. Down in the busy courtyard the hens stopped cackling. The princess's dog stopped chasing the cook's cat. In his study the King was writing his daughter's birthday card but the pen fell from his fingers. Even the kitchen fire stopped burning. The whole palace went to sleep.

Years slowly passed. The palace was forgotten. But a hundred years later a handsome young prince happened to ride by. He noticed a thorny hedge growing high in the distance. His servants laughed and told him an old story of an enchanted palace and a sleeping beauty. "But what if it's true?" the prince thought and rode towards the hedge.

At first he could see no way through. The hedge was far too thick and thorny for climbing. Then he drew his sword and began to hack his way in. The prince couldn't believe what he found on the far side. All round him animals and people stood and lay as still as statues. He walked through the palace. Not even a fly buzzed on the sunlit windows. No one moved. No one answered his questions.

Then he came to a half-open door at the base of a tower. Inside was a staircase. The prince thought he saw something gold glinting at the top. He bounded up the steps and a moment later was beside the princess. "Sleeping Beauty," he murmured to himself, leaning over her. He couldn't resist. He bent down and kissed her on the lips.

At once the princess opened her eyes. As she did so, the fire roared back into life down in the kitchen. In his study the King picked up the pen he'd dropped and finished writing his daughter's birthday card. The hens pecked for grain in the dust.

And in the room at the top of the tower, the princess saw the prince's face above her. For the first time in a hundred years she smiled. "Will you marry me?" the prince whispered. "Yes!" the princess said, and she kissed him back. When the King heard the good news, he ordered an *enormous* feast. The prince and princess were married and they lived happily ever after.